Dear Parents:

Congratulations! Your child is taking the first steps on an exciting journey. The destination? Independent reading!

STEP INTO READING® will help your child get there. The program offers five steps to reading success. Each step includes fun stories and colorful art or photographs. In addition to original fiction and books with favorite characters, there are Step into Reading Non-Fiction Readers, Phonics Readers and Boxed Sets, Sticker Readers, and Comic Readers—a complete literacy program with something to interest every child.

Learning to Read, Step by Step!

P9-DCD-426

Ready to Read   Preschool–Kindergarten
• big type and easy words • rhyme and rhythm • picture clues
For children who know the alphabet and are eager to begin reading.

Reading with Help   Preschool–Grade 1
• basic vocabulary • short sentences • simple stories
For children who recognize familiar words and sound out new words with help.

Reading on Your Own   Grades 1–3
• engaging characters • easy-to-follow plots • popular topics
For children who are ready to read on their own.

Reading Paragraphs   Grades 2–3
• challenging vocabulary • short paragraphs • exciting stories
For newly independent readers who read simple sentences with confidence.

Ready for Chapters   Grades 2–4
• chapters • longer paragraphs • full-color art
For children who want to take the plunge into chapter books but still like colorful pictures.

STEP INTO READING® is designed to give every child a successful reading experience. The grade levels are only guides; children will progress through the steps at their own speed, developing confidence in their reading.

Remember, a lifetime love of reading starts with a single step!

DISNEY · PIXAR

CARS 3

Back on Track

by Susan Amerikaner

illustrated by the Disney Storybook Art Team

Random House 🏠 New York

Lightning McQueen
is one of the
greatest racers
of all time.

He is faster than fast.

He is speed!

Sterling owns the new
Rust-eze Racing Center.

He is a big fan
of Lightning McQueen!

Cruz Ramirez
trains race cars.
She dreams of
racing one day.

Lightning is out of shape.

Cruz trains him.

She wants to make him

a great racer again.

Mack is a big truck.
He drives Lightning
all over the country.

Luigi and Guido are part of Lightning's pit crew. Luigi chooses tires. Guido changes them.

Jackson Storm is
a new kind
of race car.
He is young.
He is fast.
He keeps winning.

He even beats
Lightning!

Doc Hudson was
a great racer.
He taught Lightning
to love racing.

Lightning watches
old movies
of Doc racing.
Lightning misses Doc.

Smokey was
Doc Hudson's crew chief.
Now he trains Lightning
for the next big race.

Lightning is not
as fast as he was.
He must race smarter.

Mr. Drippy
waters the track
at Thunder Hollow.

Miss Fritter is queen
of the Thunder Hollow
Crazy Eight Derby.
She loves
to crash.

Darrell calls the action
at the Piston Cup.
Chick Hicks was a racer.
Now he has a TV show.

Natalie Certain is a guest
on Chick's show.
She says Jackson Storm
will win.

Louise Nash
was a racing star
long ago.

Now she gives Cruz
racing tips.

Cruz races.

Her dream comes true.

She is happy that

Lightning is her teammate!